Alma Flor Ada   F. Isabel Campoy

Celebrate
Mardi Gras
with Joaquín, Harlequin

Illustrated by **Eugenia Nobati**

ALFAGUARA

Today is Mardi Gras.
The whole city is dressed
in gold, purple, and green,
just like Joaquín!

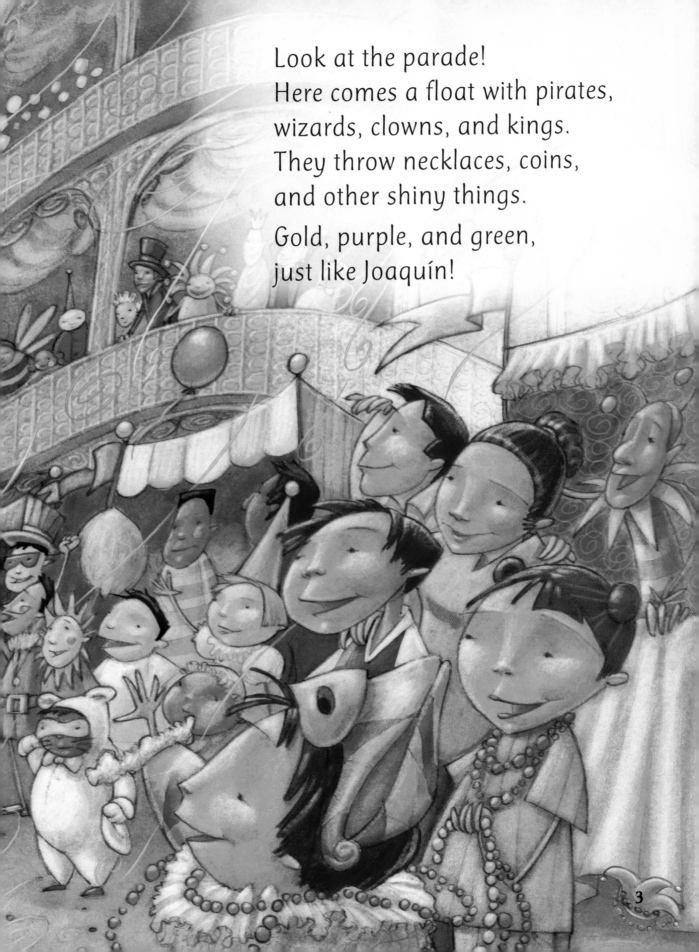

Look at the parade!
Here comes a float with pirates,
wizards, clowns, and kings.
They throw necklaces, coins,
and other shiny things.

Gold, purple, and green,
just like Joaquín!

The band is here!
Ba-ba bop, bop, bop.
Boo-boo-boop-toot-toot.
Ba-ba-bop, toot, toot.

Violin, trumpet, guitar.
Guitar, trumpet, violin.
Where is Joaquín?

"We have to find Joaquín!" shouts his mother.

"Come, Joaquín!" says Simón.

"I am not Joaquín! I'm a harlequin," says the boy.

"You may be a harlequin,
but you are my brother too.
You don't fool me, Joaquín!"

"Joaquín, I found you!" says Pilar.

"I am not Joaquín! I'm a harlequin," says the boy.

"You may be a harlequin,
but you are my brother too.
You don't fool me, Joaquín!"

"Attention, please!
We have a lost boy here.
He's dressed like a harlequin
like others we've seen,
gold, purple, and green."

Four children dressed like harlequins
but only one can be Joaquín!
So much has happened in one day!
Now they can have fun and play.

12

माँ – "Mom" in Hindi, pronounced "ma"

媽 – "Mom" in Chinese, pronounced "ma"

Maman – "Mom" in French, pronounced "ma-maw"

Is it time for something sweet?
There's a King Cake. Come and eat!
One slice has a lucky charm.
Which one could it be?
Gold?
Purple?
Green?

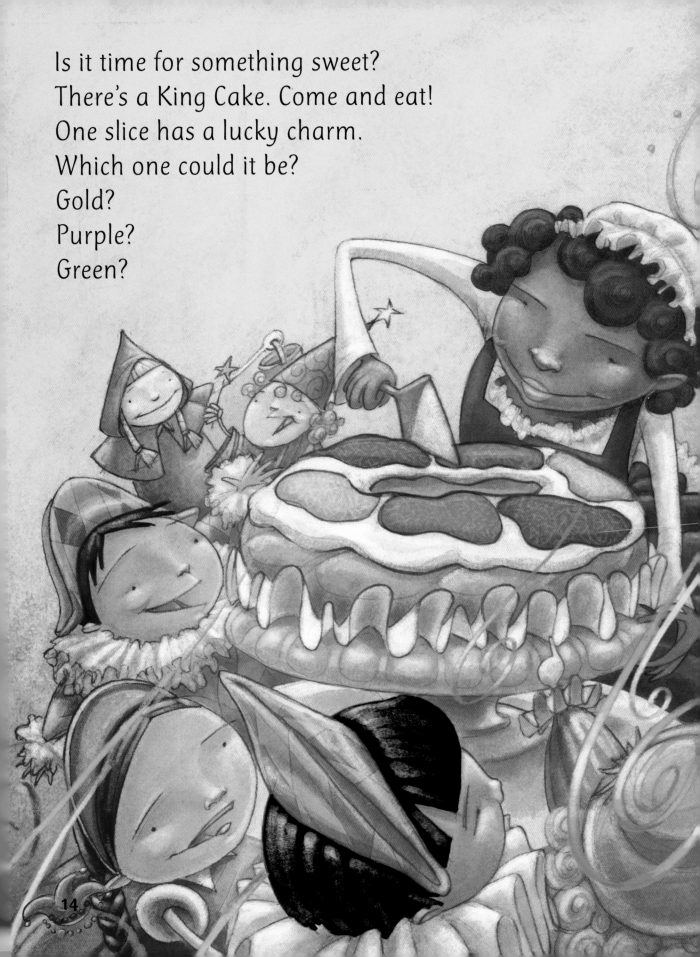

What is Mardi Gras?

"Mardi Gras"

means "fat Tuesday" in French.
Mardi Gras is a carnival. That's a big costume
party in the street! It can last many days.

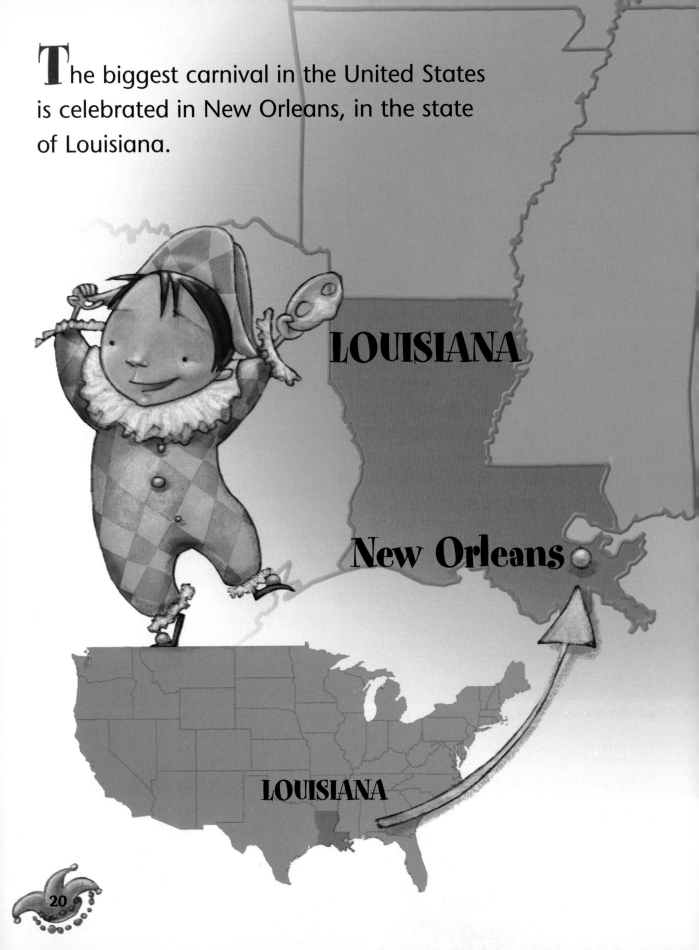

The biggest carnival in the United States is celebrated in New Orleans, in the state of Louisiana.

LOUISIANA

New Orleans

LOUISIANA

These floats parade in the streets of New Orleans.
People throw candies and necklaces from the floats.
They throw fake coins made of metal and chocolate, too.
Everyone wants to catch them!

Musicians and dancers are everywhere! They make the carnival fun. Many people come to see them.

The best part
of the carnival is
wearing a costume.

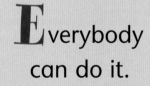

Everybody
can do it.

You and your friends can wear the same costume.

Or, you can wear an unusual costume—one that no one else has!

Even if you don't wear a costume, you will still have fun. There is a lot to see, no doubt about it!

United States
Mardi Gras Carnival in New Orleans, Louisiana
Photo by Philip Gould
© Philip Gould/CORBIS

United States
Parade of the Zulus, Mardi Gras Carnival in New Orleans, Louisiana
Photo by Dave Fornell
© Bettmann/CORBIS

Guadeloupe
Carnival in Basse-Terre
Photo by Philip Gould
© Philip Gould/CORBIS

Brazil
Carnival in Rio de Janeiro
Photo by Claudio Edinger
© Claudio Edinger/CORBIS

Brazil
Carnival in Rio de Janeiro
Photo by Earl Kowall
© Earl & Nazima Korwall/CORBIS

Trinidad and Tobago
Carnival in Port of Spain, Trinidad
Photo by Pablo Corral Vega
© Pablo Corral V/CORBIS

Bolivia
Carnival in Oruro
Photo by Anders Ryman
© Anders Ryman/CORBIS

United States
Children from Richmond, Virginia, wearing Mardi Gras masks
Photo by Lynda Richardson
© Lynda Richardson/CORBIS

Trinidad and Tobago
Carnival in Port of Spain, Trinidad
Photo by Pablo Corral Vega
© Pablo Corral V/CORBIS

United States
Mardi Gras Carnival in New Orleans, Louisiana
Photo by Joseph Sohm
© Joseph Sohm; ChromoSohm Inc./CORBIS

Trinidad and Tobago
Carnival in Port of Spain, Trinidad
Photo by Alison Wright
© Alison Wright/CORBIS

United States
Mardi Gras Carnival in New Orleans, Louisiana
Photo by Joseph Sohm
© Joseph Sohm; ChromoSohm Inc./CORBIS

Just as this book was to be sent to the printer on August 29, 2005, Hurricane Katrina devastated many towns and cities on the Gulf of Mexico, including New Orleans. Our hearts, which had celebrated the joy and cultural riches of New Orleans in these pages, were filled with deep sorrow.

We wish to dedicate this book to all the boys and girls who suffered and are still suffering in the aftermath of this tragedy, and to their families, who will always carry their beautiful city's vibrant spirit wherever they are.

We hope the smiles, art, and music New Orleans has so generously given the world will soon return. Jazz will be forever more forlorn, and forever more true.

Alma Flor Ada and F. Isabel Campoy

The Authors and the Publisher will donate a portion of the proceeds from the sales of this book to help the child survivors of Hurricane Katrina.

© This edition:
2006, Santillana USA Publishing Company, Inc.
2023 NW 84th Avenue
Miami, FL 33122
www.santillanausa.com

Text © 2006 Alma Flor Ada and F. Isabel Campoy

Managing Editor: Isabel C. Mendoza
Copyeditor: Eileen Robinson
Art Director: Mónica Candelas

Alfaguara is part of the Santillana Group, with offices in the following countries:

ARGENTINA, BOLIVIA, BRASIL, CHILE, COLOMBIA, COSTA RICA, DOMINICAN REPUBLIC, ECUADOR,
EL SALVADOR, GUATEMALA, MEXICO, PANAMA, PARAGUAY, PERU, PORTUGAL, PUERTO RICO, SPAIN,
UNITED STATES, URUGUAY, AND VENEZUELA

Celebrate Mardi Gras with Joaquín, Harlequin
ISBN 10: 1-59820-128-X
ISBN 13: 978-1-59820-128-4

Published in the United States of America
Printed in Colombia by D'vinni S.A.

15 14 13 12 11   4 5 6 7 8 9 10

Library of Congress Cataloging-in-Publication Data

Ada, Alma Flor.
    Celebrate Mardi Gras with Joaquín, Harlequin / Alma Flor Ada,
F. Isabel Campoy; illustrated by Eugenia Nobati.
      p. cm. — (Stories to celebrate)
    ISBN 1-59820-128-X
    1. Carnival—Juvenile literature. 2. Carnival—United States—
Juvenile literature. I. Campoy, F. Isabel. II. Title. III. Series.

GT4180.A33 2006
394.25—dc22   2005028751